JACK
and the
BEANSTALK

Illustrated by Lloyd Birmingham

Modern Publishing
A Division of Unisystems, Inc.
New York, New York 10022

Long ago there lived a poor widow and her son, Jack.
One summer morning their only cow, Milky White,
stopped giving milk. Jack and his mother now had no
food or money.

"We have no choice, Jack," his mother said sadly.
"You'll have to take Milky White to market and sell her."

Along the way, Jack met a funny-looking old man who offered to trade him some beans for the cow.

"These are *special* beans," said the man. "Plant them, and they'll grow so fast, they'll feed you for the rest of your life!"

And with that, Jack traded the cow for the beans. Jack held the beans tightly in his hand and he ran home as fast as he could. "Mother will be so pleased," Jack thought to himself.

Jack's mother was waiting anxiously at home. "How much did you get for Milky White?" she asked.

Jack held out the five beans triumphantly.

"Five miserable *beans?*" she wailed. "That cow was all we had to live on!"

She threw the beans out the window and burst into tears. "Off to bed without any supper, you foolish boy!"

Jack was so sad, he laid in bed and cried himself to sleep.

When Jack woke up the next morning, he couldn't believe his eyes—a huge beanstalk had sprung up overnight from the beans his mother had thrown away!

Jack hurried outdoors and started climbing up the beanstalk. He climbed and climbed, clear up to the sky!

At last, he came to a land above the clouds and saw a road stretching off in the distance.

Jack walked along the road until he came to a great big castle. And there on the doorstep stood a great big woman.

"Good morning," Jack said politely. "May I have some breakfast, please?" He was terribly hungry, not having had anything to eat the night before.

"Breakfast indeed!" said the woman. "You'll *be* breakfast if you stay around here. My husband will be home soon. He's a giant, and there's nothing he likes better than a boy grilled on toast!"

But the giant's wife took Jack to the kitchen. "You'd better eat up fast," she warned.

Jack was only half through with his porridge when the whole house began to shake. *THUMP, THUMP, THUMP!* The giant was home!

"Quick, boy, into the cupboard with you!" cried the giant's wife.

Jack barely had time to hide before the huge, nasty-looking giant came stomping into the kitchen.

The giant sniffed with his big nose. Then he
bellowed:

> *Fee, fi, fo, fum,*
> *I smell the blood of an Englishman!*
> *Be he living or be he dead,*
> *I'll grind his bones to make my bread!*

"Nonsense, my dear," said the giant's wife. "That's
just yesterday's leftovers you're smelling. Go sit down,
and I'll get your breakfast."

When the giant had finished eating, he went to a
large chest and took out three big bags of gold and started
to count his money.

Soon his head began to nod and he fell asleep.
ZZZMMFFK!...ZZZMMFFK!...ZZZMMFFK! Every snore
was like a thunderclap.

Jack didn't wait a moment longer. He jumped out of
the cupboard, grabbed one bag of gold, and ran as fast as
he could down the road.

When he got to the beanstalk, he threw down the bag
of gold, and climbed down after it.

After the gold ran out, Jack climbed up the beanstalk again and walked to the giant's castle.

"Go away!" the giant's wife said to him.

THUMP, THUMP, THUMP! It was the giant's footsteps again!

"Quick, into the cupboard," cried the woman.

The giant gobbled up all his breakfast. Then his wife brought him his magic hen, and the giant roared, "Gold!" And the hen laid an egg made of pure gold!

As soon as the giant fell asleep, Jack jumped out of the cupboard. And before anyone could stop him, he grabbed the hen and ran to the beanstalk—lickety-split!

The very next day, Jack again climbed up the beanstalk and sneaked into the giant's castle.

Pretty soon Jack heard the giant roar. *"Fe, fi, fo fum! I smell the blood of an Englishman!"*

"There's no boy here," said his wife.

The giant finally sat down to eat, and when he was full, he told his wife, "Bring out my magic harp!"

"Play!" said the giant— and at once the gold harp began to play.

Then the giant dozed off, and Jack climbed out from behind the cupboard, grabbed the magic harp, and started to run! But as soon as Jack touched it, the harp began to shriek, *"Master! Master! Help me!"*

The giant awoke, bellowed with rage and ran after Jack.

"Quick, into the cupboard," cried the woman.

The giant gobbled up all his breakfast. Then his wife brought him his magic hen, and the giant roared, "Gold!"

And the hen laid an egg made of pure gold!

As soon as the giant fell asleep, Jack jumped out of the cupboard. And before anyone could stop him, he grabbed the hen and ran to the beanstalk—lickety-split!

The very next day, Jack again climbed up the beanstalk and sneaked into the giant's castle.

Pretty soon Jack heard the giant roar. *"Fe, fi, fo fum! I smell the blood of an Englishman!"*

"There's no boy here," said his wife.

The giant finally sat down to eat, and when he was full, he told his wife, "Bring out my magic harp!"

"Play!" said the giant— and at once the gold harp began to play.

Then the giant dozed off, and Jack climbed out from behind the cupboard, grabbed the magic harp, and started to run! But as soon as Jack touched it, the harp began to shriek, *"Master! Master! Help me!"*

The giant awoke, bellowed with rage and ran after Jack.

Jack flung himself on the beanstalk and started climbing down as fast as he could. The giant was right behind him.

"Quick, Mother! Bring the ax!" Jack yelled.

Jack started chopping with all his might! *CRA-A-ACK, BOOM!* Down crashed the giant. He fell through the ground and disappeared beneath it.

Jack and his mother became rich by selling the golden eggs, and they lived happily ever after listening to the magic harp.